DONKEY DERBY

Also in the Animal Ark Pets series

LUCY DANIELS

Donkey Derby

Illustrated by Paul Howard

Hodder
Children's
Books

a division of Hodder Headline plc

Special thanks to Wendy Douthwaite

Text copyright © 1999 Ben M. Baglio
Created by Ben M. Baglio, London W12 7QY
Illustrations copyright © 1999 Paul Howard
Cover illustration by Chris Chapman

First published in Great Britain in 1999
by Hodder Children's Books

A Catalogue record for this book is available from the British Library

ISBN 0 340 73585 6

Typeset by Avon Dataset Ltd, Bidford-on-Avon, Warks

Printed and bound in Great Britain by
The Guernsey Press Co. Ltd, Channel Isles

Hodder Children's Books
a division of Hodder Headline plc
338 Euston Road
London NW1 3BH

Contents

Contents

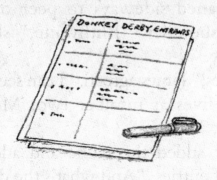

1

Entries

"Next one, James!" Mandy waited, with her pen poised above the list.

James peered at the entry form. "It's terrible writing," he said, pushing his glasses further up his nose and putting his face closer to the piece of paper. But it didn't help. He still couldn't read the name written on it. "John Bli . . . Bling . . . Oh! I give up!"

"Let me see." Nine-year-old Mandy Hope leaned sideways to peer over her friend's shoulder. "Blithwaite," she said, decisively.

"Oh yes," James agreed. "I can see it now. And he lives at number two, Moorfield Cottages, Walton."

Mandy added the name and address to the list of entries. "And what's the donkey's name?" she asked James.

"Pickles," James replied. "Or it could be Tiddles. But that sounds more like a cat!"

Mandy laughed. "I think we'll settle for Pickles," she said, writing it in.

Mandy Hope and her best friend, James Hunter, were sitting at the huge old kitchen table at Animal Ark. They were going through the entry forms for this year's Donkey Derby, which was to take place at the Welford Spring Fair. At the moment it was hard to imagine it ever happening. Rain lashed against the kitchen window, and the outside world looked grey and horrible. But Mandy didn't mind. Inside Animal Ark it was warm and cosy.

In the modern extension at the back of the cottage, Mandy's parents, Adam and Emily Hope, were finishing off Animal Ark's Saturday morning veterinary surgery.

Mandy turned her attention back to the matter in hand. "I don't know John Blithwaite *or* Pickles," she admitted. "They must go to another vet."

James nodded. "For some reason there are quite a lot of new names entered for this year's Donkey Derby," he said. "Some are from outside Welford, too."

"Hmm. It *is* rather strange, isn't it?" Mandy replied. "Last year there were only a few entries – no more than a handful. Yet, *this* year, we have masses of entries already! I wonder why."

James shrugged. "It's good, though, isn't it?" he said. "More people paying to enter their donkeys in the race means more money for the Glisterdale Horse and Pony Rescue Sanctuary."

"Exactly," Mandy said. "They need all the money they can get!" Mandy loved animals. So did James. And that was why they were such good friends. The two of them spent as much time as they could helping animals in need.

"Talking of Glisterdale," James said, "it will be odd having a Donkey Derby without Lightning this year, won't it?"

"It certainly will!" Mandy agreed. Lightning the donkey lived at Glisterdale and for the last few years had always won the Derby. But this year she was expecting a foal, so she had to take things easy.

Mandy looked down at the list in front of her. "It's great that Dad's letting us sort out the entries for him, isn't it?" she said. "Being the race organiser, he usually does it himself. But he and Mum are extra-busy at the moment, with Simon being away." Simon, the practice's veterinary nurse, was on holiday.

Just then, Adam Hope burst in. His vet's bag was in his hand and he looked like he was in a hurry. "How are you doing, you two?" he asked.

"Fine, Dad," Mandy replied. "Surgery finished?"

4

Mr Hope nodded. "Mum's just finishing with her last patient." He held up his bag. "I'm going off to Blackheath Farm now. Tom Masters is worried about his hens. Then I'll have to rush back and see to the animals in the residential unit." Mr Hope ran his fingers through his hair. "Phew!" He laughed. "I'll be glad when Simon's back!" Simon usually took care of the animals in the residential unit next to the surgery.

"Poor Dad!" Mandy said. "I wish I could help out." Mandy longed to help with the sick animals in the residential unit, but her mum and dad said that she must wait until she was twelve. That was three years away!

Adam Hope came over and gave his daughter a hug. "You and James *are* helping, love," he replied, "by listing all the Donkey Derby entries for me. It'll make my job as race organiser much easier!"

Pulling on his coat, Mr Hope grinned. "I must dash," he said, "but ask Mum where she's going when she's finished with her last patient . . ." he continued, his eyes

twinkling. "A little bird told me that she's off to the rescue sanctuary. It seems that Lightning is about to have her foal. If you ask nicely, maybe she'll take you and James with her."

James jumped up from the table, smiling broadly. "Great!" he said. "Do you think your mum would let us watch the foal being born? That would be brilliant!"

"I'm being talked about," said Mrs Hope, coming into the room. "Nothing bad, I hope." She smiled as she quickly combed her long red hair and tied it back with a stretchy cotton band.

"Can we, Mum?" Mandy asked, excitedly. "Can we come to see Lightning's foal?" Mandy loved Lightning. James was right: it wouldn't be the same at the Donkey Derby without her. But how exciting to see her foal!

"Hold on, hold on," said Mrs Hope, laughing, "Lightning hasn't had it yet!" She reached for her coat. "Right then, it sounds like we're *all* going!"

"We've got lots of entries for the Donkey Derby," Mandy told her mother as they bounced along the main road in the Animal Ark Land-rover. "Much more than last year. There were only about six donkeys then; this year we've got eighteen already! Why do you think that is, Mum?"

"Well," Mrs Hope replied, "I should think it's because Lightning won't be running." She slowed for a bend in the road. "She's the fastest donkey I've ever seen," Mrs Hope explained. "She's won the Welford Donkey

Derby every year since she arrived at Glisterdale five years ago. Perhaps other owners stopped entering their donkeys because they knew Lightning was faster, and would win. But this year is different."

Mandy grabbed James's arm. "Of course!" she said. "Lightning won't be able to enter, because she'll be too busy with her new foal—"

"So the other owners think that their donkey might stand a chance this year!" James finished.

Mandy thought for a moment. "But what about poor Mel?" Melanie Dawkins was the same age as Mandy and was the grand-daughter of Joyce Dawkins, who owned Glisterdale. Mel always stayed with her gran during spring half-term, when the Fair was held. She loved the Donkey Derby.

James looked at Mandy. "What do you mean, 'poor Mel'?"

"Well," Mandy explained, "Mel has always wanted to ride Lightning in the Donkey Derby, and last year Mrs Dawkins agreed that she was old enough. Then Mel broke her arm and she couldn't ride. So her gran promised her that she could ride *this* year." Mandy sighed. "Poor Mel," she said again. "When she wrote to me at Christmas, she was *already* excited about taking part in the Donkey Derby."

"There's always next year," Mrs Hope said, peering through the rain-splattered windscreen.

Mandy thought the windscreen wipers, swishing backwards and forwards, looked like two happy dogs' tails. "But she'll be too old to ride a donkey soon, if much more happens!" she replied.

Mrs Hope slowed the Land-rover down to a crawl. "Here we are," she said. She turned off the main road and began the gentle climb up the twisting lane leading to Glisterdale Horse and Pony Rescue Sanctuary.

Joyce Dawkins was waiting for them, and looking rather anxious. The large, friendly woman gave a smile of relief as Emily emerged from the Land-rover. Welcoming them all, she led them hurriedly into Lightning's stable. Mandy and James's eyes opened wide when they saw the donkey.

Joyce laughed. "She looks a little different to when you saw her winning the Derby last year, doesn't she?"

"Er . . . yes . . . just a bit," they both said politely. Lightning looked *enormous*!

"She'll be back to her old self soon, though. Won't you, sweetie?" said Mrs Hope. She spoke in a soothing voice as she tried to examine Lightning. The donkey was moving about restlessly.

"She can't keep still," Joyce Dawkins explained.

Mrs Hope managed to get Lightning to stay in one place, and Mandy went over to see if she could help to calm the donkey down.

She stroked Lightning's face while her mother finished her examination. "You're going to be a clever girl, aren't you, Lightning?" Mandy crooned to the little donkey. "You're going to have a lovely foal. And Mum's here, so you'll be fine."

Emily Hope straightened up and smiled. "Thanks, love," she said to Mandy, then she looked over at Mrs Dawkins. "I think we arrived just in time, Joyce." She smiled. "It won't be long before Lightning is a mum!"

Just as Mrs Hope was speaking, Mandy felt Lightning's head pull away. The donkey slowly lowered herself down on to the straw.

"Here we go!" said Mrs Hope cheerfully.

2
Lightning's foal

"Mum!" squeaked Mandy. "It's coming!"

Mrs Hope watched Lightning carefully. The donkey grunted as a tiny head appeared below her tail. Two tiny donkey ears. Two tiny front legs. Lightning gave another long grunt, and the foal slid out from her body and on to the straw. The baby donkey was perfect. Tiny, black and slippery wet – but perfect.

James gasped in wonder. All Mandy could say was, "Oh, Mum!" Her mother smiled across the stable at her, and Mandy knew she understood how she felt.

Emily Hope stood by, but Lightning didn't seem to need much help. "Well," she commented, with a chuckle, "Lightning by name and lightning by nature. That *was* quick!"

"Are they both all right?" Joyce Dawkins asked, her face still looking a little anxious.

"They're just fine, Joyce," Mrs Hope replied, after she'd listened to the foal's heart and lungs with her stethoscope. "Lightning has a darling jenny foal. She's a little small – but healthy and beautiful, just like her mother. And maybe," Mrs Hope joked, "if she can come into the world that quickly, she'll be as fast as Lightning in the Donkey Derby!"

Joyce Dawkins beamed with pleasure. "Wonderful!"

Lightning began to stand up. Mandy watched as her mother fixed clamps in two places on the cord that joined Lightning to her foal. Expertly, Emily Hope then cut the cord. The baby was on her own. A tiny new creature.

Lightning seemed to know exactly what to do. She turned her head and began to lick her foal. Very gently, she licked off the shining fluid that covered her baby.

Mandy turned to Joyce Dawkins. "What will you call her?" she asked.

"Well, I thought of the name yesterday," Mrs Dawkins replied. "And now I've seen her, it seems perfect. Just look on her forehead. She's got a white splash, just like a raindrop. That's what I'll call her – Raindrop!"

"Oh, that's a lovely name," said Mandy. "Especially since it's raining today! Isn't that great, James?"

James nodded. "Look!" he said to Mandy, pointing to the foal.

As they watched, Raindrop began to push shakily on her two front hooves and lift herself up a little. She sat up in the straw, her two spindly front legs wobbling.

Lightning continued to lick her new foal carefully.

Mandy gasped again as Raindrop then began to struggle to her feet. Gradually, Lightning nudged her baby closer. Tottering on her long thin legs at her mother's side, Raindrop lifted her head and began to feed from her mother's teat.

They all watched in silence for a moment. Then Joyce Dawkins sighed. "I'm so pleased they're both doing so well," she said. "My only problem now is how to tell Melanie . . ."

"Oh," James said. "So she still doesn't know about Lightning having a foal?"

Mrs Dawkins shook her head. "I promised her she really could ride Lightning in the Donkey Derby this year. I've been putting off disappointing her," she admitted.

Mandy looked at her. "But when Mel finds out *why* she can't ride Lightning she'll be fine. She'll *love* Raindrop. And she'll be so proud of Lightning!"

Mrs Dawkins smiled uncertainly. "Do you really think so, dear?" she said. "I do hope

you are right . . . But I think I'll wait until Melanie gets here. Then she can see for herself."

Mandy was still thinking about the donkeys at breakfast on Monday morning.

"I wonder how they're doing?" she said to her mother, as she poured milk on to her cereal.

"Who?" asked Mrs Hope.

"Lightning and Raindrop, of course," Mandy replied.

"Of course," her mother said, laughing. "I might have guessed!" She pushed back her chair and began to clear the table. "I'm going to see them today," she said.

"Ooh, Mum!" Mandy said. "Can I come? Please don't go until school's finished. And can James come, too?"

Emily Hope grinned at her daughter. "I suppose I could just about have time to pick you and James up from school, visit Glisterdale and still be back in time for the start of evening surgery."

"Brilliant!" Mandy beamed.

Mrs Hope looked at the kitchen clock. "I'll give Mrs Hunter a quick ring to make sure it's OK for James to come with us to Glisterdale, but while I'm doing that, young lady, you'd better get ready for school – if you don't get a move on, you'll be late!"

Mandy jumped up from the table, gave her mum a quick kiss and took her empty bowl over to the sink. "Thanks, Mum," she said, and went to fetch her schoolbag from her bedroom.

When she came back downstairs, her mother was just hanging up the phone. "James's mum says that's fine," Mrs Hope said, "so I'll meet you both after school. I'll park as near as I can to the school gates. Try to be on time!"

James was waiting for Mandy in his usual spot by the old oak tree on the village green. Mandy rushed up to him a few minutes later. "Sorry I'm a bit late," she puffed.

"I'd nearly given up on you," James replied. "What took you so long?"

Mandy quickly explained about the visit

to Glisterdale after school.

"Great," James said. "I'm on for that."

As they started walking in the direction of school, James pulled a piece of paper out of his bag. "I was busy on my computer last night," he told Mandy, pushing his glasses further up his nose. "I hope you like it," he said. "I thought we could put it on the school bulletin board."

Mandy looked at the poster. It read:

WELFORD SPRING FAIR
including the
DONKEY DERBY
at 3 p.m.
(Entry forms from Animal Ark
Veterinary Surgery.)

"Oh, James, that's great!" Mandy said. She thought for a moment, then asked, "And you could print off more, couldn't you? We could put them all round the village as well."

"That's what I thought," agreed James. "After we've visited Lightning and

Raindrop, we can go to my house to print off some more posters and collect Blackie. He can come with us and have a walk while we're going around putting up the posters."

"Great plan!" said Mandy happily, as they walked through the school gates. She couldn't wait until later!

The Animal Ark Land–rover was parked by the school gates when Mandy and James came out.

"I wonder if Raindrop has grown," Mandy said, heaving herself up into the high seat next to her mother. James climbed in behind her and slammed the door shut.

"I'm sure she'll have grown a little bit, love – but not enough for you to notice. Not in just two days!" Emily Hope replied, laughing. "I'll weigh her again, though," she added, as she started up the Land–rover and pulled away. "She should have put on a little weight."

The journey passed quite quickly as Mandy and James told Mrs Hope what they'd been doing at school that day. Before long they were driving back up the twisting lane that led to Glisterdale.

Joyce Dawkins led them into Lightning and Raindrop's stable, and straight away Mandy could see that Raindrop looked stronger. She stroked the little foal's soft, dark coat, and Raindrop pushed her tiny velvety nose into Mandy's hand. "She's so gorgeous," Mandy said. Lightning looked on, happily.

Emily Hope went to stand beside Mrs Dawkins. "Mother and daughter are looking well," she said, smiling. "Lightning seems to be a good mother." She reached into her bag for her portable scales.

Mandy and James made a fuss of Lightning while Mrs Hope weighed the foal. Lightning's belly seemed to have shrunk a little now that her foal had been born. But the donkey was still a bit plumper than when she had galloped past the winning post at last year's Donkey Derby. This reminded Mandy about Mel. "When is Mel coming, Mrs Dawkins?" she asked.

"On Saturday," Joyce Dawkins replied.

"I'm picking her up from the train station in Walton."

"I'm really looking forward to seeing her again," Mandy said. She smiled as she watched her mum lift Raindrop from the scales and let her totter on her long spindly legs back to Lightning. "So, has Raindrop put on any weight?" she asked.

"Over half a kilogramme!" Mrs Hope replied. "She's doing really well." She turned to Joyce Dawkins. "Right then, Joyce, I need to rush back for evening

surgery now, but I'll pop over on Saturday afternoon." She looked at Mandy and James. "I imagine I might have company then, too – especially if Mel is arriving!"

Mandy and James nodded an enthusiastic agreement.

"Absolutely," said James.

Mrs Dawkins laughed. "You're more than welcome," she said. "I'm sure Mel would love to catch up with you."

Mandy kissed Raindrop's nose and gave Lightning a quick pat. "We'll see you again on Saturday," she told them.

They all trooped out to the Land-rover.

"If all is well on Saturday, I don't think you'll need me for a while," Emily Hope told Mrs Dawkins. "So the next time I'll see you after that will be at the Spring Fair!"

WELFORD SPRING FAIR
including the
DONKEY DERBY
at 3 p.m.
(Entry forms from Animal Ark Veterinary Surgery)

3
More donkeys

On the way back from Glisterdale, Mandy
and James told Mrs Hope about the poster.
She thought it was a great idea, and dropped
them off at James's house.

"I'll leave my schoolbag with you, Mum,"
Mandy said, as she and James climbed out
of the Land-rover. She turned to James. "I
can carry the posters in your bag, James.

You'll have enough to do, dealing with Blackie!"

James's black Labrador puppy, Blackie, was very lively. He was the reason that Mandy and James had met – and as they had become such good friends, James had said that Mandy could share Blackie. Mandy couldn't have any pets of her own, as there were already so many animals to be taken care of at Animal Ark.

As Mandy followed James down the drive, he turned to grin at her. "Blackie didn't have a very long walk this morning," he explained, "so get ready to be jumped on!"

Mandy could hear Blackie barking. "He's heard us!" she said, laughing. James led the way round the side of the house to the back door. Blackie was at the kitchen window, his paws on the windowsill. His tail was waving as fast as it possibly could.

James opened the back door. "Now steady, Blackie," James began. "There's a good—" But all Blackie's training was forgotten, as he jumped up at them, barking excitedly.

★ ★ ★

A few minutes later, armed with more posters printed from James's computer and some biscuits to keep them going until teatime, Mandy and James were ready to go again.

James clipped Blackie's lead to his collar, and was soon being pulled along towards the village green.

James let Blackie have a good run while Mandy pinned a poster on the wide trunk of the old oak tree by the village pond. Next, they pinned a poster on the notice board near Welford Church, then made their way to the post office.

Mandy loved the post office. It was run by Mrs McFarlane, and was also a general store. Mrs McFarlane seemed to sell almost everything that anyone could ever need. But when you went into the shop you had to be careful not to knock things off the crowded shelves – especially when Blackie and his constantly wagging tail were with you, as there wasn't much room left for customers!

The doorbell pinged as Mandy pushed

open the door and went inside, followed
by James and Blackie. Mandy could see Mrs
McFarlane behind her little post–office
cubby–hole, to the side of the shop counter.
She was busy with some forms, and getting
ready to close, but as soon as she saw the
two of them and Blackie she came bustling
out.

"Well, well, and here's that lovely
Blackie," Mrs McFarlane said, bending
down to fuss the puppy, who wriggled with
pleasure. "And how are his collar and lead

doing?" she asked James. When Blackie was very young, Mandy had gone with James to Mrs McFarlane's shop to buy him his smart red collar and lead.

"He's growing so much that the collar's on the loosest hole, Mrs McFarlane," James replied proudly. He pushed his glasses further up on his nose. "I'll have to buy him a new one, soon."

"Well, he's a fine, healthy dog," Mrs McFarlane said. "And how can I help you today?" she asked them.

Mandy showed her the poster. "We're trying to get as much support for the Donkey Derby as we possibly can, so we thought we'd put up some posters in the village."

Mrs McFarlane looked at the poster. "That's a fine idea," she said. "And I guess you'd like me to put one up on the post-office notice board?" she asked.

"That's right," James said, trying to stop Blackie from investigating the pile of newspapers nearby. "If you've got room, that is."

"I'll *make* room," Mrs McFarlane said, smiling. "I'd like to see the Spring Fair well supported. It's for a good cause."

As Mandy and James left the post office, they spotted Mrs Edwards outside her greengrocer's shop, packing up for the day. Tilly, her Corgi dog, was bustling at her feet. She took a poster for her window. "Let's hope we have a nice sunny day for it!" she said, cheerily.

"Just one left for the notice board in the Animal Ark waiting-room," Mandy said, as she and James parted and went their separate ways home for tea.

The following day at school, Rachel Lowe came up to Mandy and James in the playground. Mandy didn't know Rachel very well. She was a rather shy, quiet girl in James's class. She and her parents hadn't lived in Welford for long.

But today Rachel seemed to have lost her shyness. She seemed really excited about something. "You live at Animal Ark, don't you?" she said to Mandy.

Mandy smiled and nodded.

"I've just seen the poster on the school bulletin board about the Spring Fair and Donkey Derby," Rachel continued. "It said to contact Animal Ark. Well, *I've* got a donkey!" she said, her eyes shining. "She's called Truffle. And we'd *love* to enter! Truffle's really fast when she gets going!"

Mandy beamed at Rachel. "Great!" she said. "Truffle's a lovely name," she added.

"Well, she's a sort of chocolatey–brown colour − like a chocolate truffle!" Rachel explained. "And she's really gentle and quiet."

"I can bring you an entry form tomorrow, if you like," Mandy offered.

"Yes, please," Rachel replied.

"One more for our list," James said, smiling, as the school bell rang. "See you at home time."

The next day, Mandy took a Donkey Derby entry form to school. At breaktime she gave it to Rachel.

"Thanks a lot," Rachel said, smiling at

Mandy. Then her face clouded, and she bit her lip. "There's just one thing . . ." she began.

"What's the matter?" Mandy asked. She could see that Rachel was worried about something.

"It's my dog, Maisie," Rachel told her. "She's a lurcher. She's having pups."

"But that's great!" Mandy said. She looked puzzled. "So why are you worried? She's all right, isn't she?"

"Well, yes, she seems fine," Rachel said.

"But, you see, Maisie looks as though she is due to have her pups *soon*! What if she starts having her pups on the day of the Donkey Derby?"

"Oh . . . I see," Mandy said. "That could be difficult, couldn't it?" Mandy thought hard. "Well," she said, at last, "why don't you bring Maisie to the surgery at Animal Ark? Mum or Dad can examine her to make sure everything's all right, and maybe they can tell you when Maisie's likely to give birth."

Rachel cheered up. "Will they be able to tell from examining her?"

Mandy nodded. "I'm pretty sure they can," she replied.

"OK, then," Rachel said. "I'll ask Mum to make an appointment." She smiled at Mandy. "*And* I'll enter Truffle in the Donkey Derby!"

4

Maisie

It was Saturday, the first day of half-term. James had just phoned to say that he was coming over. Mandy's dad had already gone out on a visit, and her mum was off to Glisterdale as soon as morning surgery finished. Mandy couldn't wait to see Mel again – as well as Lightning and Raindrop!

Mandy opened the door leading into the

Animal Ark waiting-room. There were only a few owners with their pets this morning. *Great!* she thought. *We'll be able to get off to Glisterdale pretty soon!*

Then Mandy heard a thumping sound. She turned towards the noise. Molly, a black Labrador from Moorcroft Farm, was lying at the feet of Mrs Lawson, her owner. Molly was Blackie's mother. Her tail was wagging against the floor of the waiting-room.

"Molly!" Mandy hurried over and bent down to the Labrador. "Hello, girl," she said, tickling her behind the ears. She noticed that one of Molly's front paws was bandaged. Mandy looked up anxiously at Molly's owner. "Hello, Mrs Lawson. What has Molly done to her paw?"

Mrs Lawson looked down at her dog. "She's cut her foot quite badly on some glass," she explained. "I've bathed it, of course, but I'd like your mum to have a look. I think Molly will need some antibiotics."

Just then, the examination-room door opened. Emily Hope appeared; she was showing Mrs Edwards and Tilly out. Jean Knox, the receptionist, beckoned to Mrs Lawson to go in.

Mrs Hope caught sight of Mandy. "Won't be long, love," she called, smiling at her daughter. "Now, Mrs Lawson, what can we do for you and Molly, here?"

As the door closed behind Mrs Lawson and Molly, Mandy turned to Mrs Edwards and Tilly, who were on their way out through reception. Mrs Edwards looked in a hurry, but her Corgi wagged her stump of a tail at Mandy and pulled back towards her.

"What's wrong with Tilly, Mrs Edwards?" Mandy asked.

"A bit of skin trouble, dear," she replied. "Your mum's given me some lotion and a special shampoo. I'm sure it'll be better soon." She pulled at Tilly's lead. "Can't stay now, dear," she explained. "I've got to get back to the shop! Must rush!"

She was about to hurry away, but then she hesitated and turned back round to Mandy. "By the way, I've told my nephew George out at Monkton Spinney about your poster. He's got a donkey – so I've picked up an entry form for him. Goodbye for now!" And Mrs Edwards was gone, with Tilly pattering obediently along behind her.

Mandy smiled to herself. It was good to know that because of the posters there were already *two* extra donkeys who might be racing in the Donkey Derby!

Back in the waiting-room Jean smiled at Mandy. She put on her glasses, which were dangling on a chain around her neck. "I see that your mum is off to Glisterdale after morning surgery," she said, with a twinkle in her eye. "I don't suppose you're waiting to go with her, by any chance?" she joked. She began to tidy up the papers on her desk. "I hear Lightning's foal is gorgeous."

Mandy nodded. She was just about to tell Jean all about Raindrop when the surgery door opened and a dog's face appeared. It was a long, thin face, with beautiful, gentle eyes. The door opened further, and in came the rest of the dog, followed by Rachel Lowe and a woman Mandy presumed was her mother.

"Oh, hi, Rachel," Mandy said, smiling. "This must be Maisie." She went over to stroke the lurcher. "She's beautiful, isn't she?" Mandy said. "And not very fat," she added, "considering she's about to have puppies!"

Rachel smiled. "You should see her when she's not expecting," she said. "Lurchers are really thin dogs."

Rachel and her mother settled themselves on two chairs at the side of the waiting-room, and Maisie lay down quietly at

Rachel's feet. Rachel introduced her mother to Mandy, and Mandy was just about to ask about Truffle when the examination-room door opened again. Mrs Lawson came out, with Molly limping behind her. Molly had a clean white bandage around her paw.

"It'll soon heal up, now," Emily Hope was saying. "Start her on the tablets straight away, won't you?" Taking details of the next patient from Jean, Mrs Hope then turned to Rachel and her mother. "Mrs Lowe . . . and Rachel," she said, smiling. "Do come in. And Maisie, of course."

The door closed, and Mandy turned to Molly. She bent down to stroke the Labrador. "You'll soon feel better, Molly," she told her. "I'll send your love to Blackie, shall I?"

Molly wagged her tail and barked, and Mrs Lawson laughed. "I think she understood you, Mandy," she said, as she left the waiting-room with Molly.

Mandy told Jean Knox about Raindrop while she waited for Rachel to come out of the examination room. At last, the door opened and Rachel's mother emerged, followed by Rachel, with Maisie on her lead.

"Is she OK?" Mandy asked, hurrying over to Rachel.

"Your mum says she's really fit," Rachel replied, beaming. "There don't seem to be any problems."

"And the date for the puppies?" Mandy asked.

"Well . . ." Rachel said, "your mum thinks the pups are due a couple of days *after* the Spring Fair."

Mandy smiled. "Good! So with any luck you'll be able to win the Donkey Derby *and* watch Maisie's puppies being born!"

"Let's hope so," Rachel laughed and she waved to Mrs Hope. Then she followed her mother out of the door, with Maisie trotting behind.

While Mrs Hope was checking the animals in the residential unit, Jean Knox put on her coat and changed the sign on the surgery door to 'Closed'. Mandy counted how many of the Donkey Derby entry forms were left underneath James's poster in the waiting-room. Most of them had gone! She had a feeling that this year's Donkey Derby was going to be *very* popular!

5

A big surprise

Before long, James had arrived, and the Animal Ark Land-rover was on its way to Glisterdale. As it pulled up in the drive outside the rescue sanctuary, Mandy noticed a car coming up behind them. "Look, Mum. It's Mrs Dawkins. And Mel! They must have just come from the train station. Great!" she added excitedly. "Now we can show Raindrop to Mel."

She opened the door and jumped out.
"Come on, James," she said, pulling at his
sleeve. "Let's go and say hello."

As Mrs Dawkins pulled up next to the
Land-rover, Mandy and James hurried
round to open the car doors for them.

Oh dear, Mandy thought, as she spotted
Mel's hard hat on the back seat. "Hi, Mel!"
she said, giving the girl a hug. "I'm so pleased
you're here again."

"Me too," said Mel. But she didn't
look very happy. Mandy wondered if
Mel had already found out she couldn't
ride Lightning in the Donkey Derby,
and was taking the news badly. She hoped
not.

Nervously pushing her shoulder-length
fair hair out of her eyes, Mel looked over
towards Emily Hope. "Is everything all
right?" she asked Mandy.

"Everything's great!" Mandy replied,
trying to sound cheerful.

Mel's grey eyes looked doubtful. "Are you
sure? Why is your mum here with her vet's

44

bag, then? Is there something wrong with Lightning?"

"Oh, I see!" Mandy said, suddenly relieved. "Lightning's fine, Mel."

Joyce Dawkins came over to her granddaughter. "Mandy's right, dear," she said. "Lightning's fine." She put an arm around Mel's shoulders. "But there's something you need to know about Lightning. Something I really should have told you. But I kept putting it off . . ."

Mel looked round at them all. "What is all this?" she asked. "You're all being very mysterious."

"Joyce," said Emily Hope, tactfully, "why don't we have that cup of tea you promised me. Mandy and James can take Mel to Lightning's stable so she can see for herself. Then they can explain."

Mrs Dawkins nodded gratefully. She picked up Mel's bags and took Emily Hope off to her kitchen.

Mandy looked at Mel. "Right!" she said, grinning. "Have *we* got a surprise for you! Come on!"

★ ★ ★

As Mandy, James and Mel reached the entrance to Lightning's stable, Mandy put her hands over Mel's eyes and James opened the door.

Mandy guided Mel through the doorway. "Now . . ." she said, "open your eyes!"

Mel did as she was asked. Lightning was standing in the straw, with Raindrop cuddled close to her side, looking back at Mel with bright, inquisitive eyes.

For a while, Mel just stood there, looking. At last, she spoke. "Wow!" she said. "Wowee!" She continued to stare for a moment. "But why didn't Gran want to tell me?" she asked Mandy.

"Well, she knew you'd be pleased about Raindrop," Mandy explained. "But because Lightning's just had a foal she won't be strong enough to enter the Donkey Derby this year." Mandy put a sympathetic hand on Mel's shoulder. "She knew you'd be disappointed about not being able to ride her."

"Oh . . . yes, of course," Mel said, in a

46

small voice. "I didn't think of that straight away. I remember Gran telling me: ponies and donkeys shouldn't be ridden if they are still making milk to feed their foals."

Mel looked across at Mandy and James. "I *am* disappointed," she admitted. "I was really looking forward to riding Lightning this year. But—" Mel looked back at Raindrop. She took a gentle step forward towards the donkey and her foal. "How could I be sorry that Raindrop has arrived?"

Mel put her arms around Lightning's neck. "Can I stroke your baby?" she asked the donkey. "Can I stroke Raindrop?"

Mandy watched as Mel squatted down and reached a hand out to Raindrop.

"Hello, little one," Mel said, softly. The little foal stretched her neck, sniffing at her. Mel smiled. "You're *adorable*, aren't you?"

Mandy heaved a sigh of relief – Mel was making the best of things and not thinking about being disappointed. They all sat in the straw for a while, just talking and watching Lightning and Raindrop.

"Let's look on the bright side," Mel said,

grinning. "At least the other donkeys at the Derby will have a chance this year!"

They all laughed.

"Do you know how Lightning came to be here at Glisterdale?" Mel asked.

Mandy and James shook their heads.

"She was a seaside donkey," Mel explained. "She loved giving rides to the children – but she just couldn't resist taking them for a *fast* ride! And of course that frightened them." Mel smiled. "Lightning just loved racing, and they couldn't stop her!"

They looked across at Lightning, who was munching contentedly, and they laughed. Looking at her now, it seemed hard to believe that the donkey could be so energetic.

"So the owners decided to send her to Glisterdale," Mel finished.

Just then, Emily Hope and Joyce Dawkins arrived in the stable. Mrs Dawkins looked anxiously at her granddaughter.

Mel leaped up and put her arms round her grandmother. "Oh, Gran!" she said. "She's beautiful!"

Mrs Dawkins hugged her granddaughter back. She looked very relieved.

Emily Hope smiled at Mandy and gave her a "thumbs-up" sign. "Right," she said, opening her bag and taking out her stethoscope. "Time to give Raindrop her check-up." She crouched in the straw beside the foal. "Can you come and hold her still for a moment please, Mandy?"

Mandy went over and put one arm around Raindrop's neck and the other round her rump. She held her gently but firmly, while

Emily Hope held the stethoscope against the foal's chest. "Her heart's fine," said the vet. Then, moving the stethoscope further over, she listened to Raindrop's lungs.

Mandy thought it was great. First, she had seen Raindrop's birth, and now she was helping with the little foal's check-up.

Mandy watched as her mother felt down Raindrop's legs. Mrs Hope checked the foal's backbone, examined her tail and looked into her tiny grey ears. Gently, she opened the baby donkey's mouth.

"Everything's still fine," Emily Hope said, at last. She stood up and turned to Lightning. "And now for Mum," she said.

Mandy watched Joyce Dawkins go over to Mel. "You don't mind too much, do you, dear?" Mrs Dawkins asked her granddaughter.

Mel put her arms round her gran's neck. "Of course I don't, Gran," she said. "It's silly to be disappointed. I mean, a baby donkey is more exciting than riding in a Donkey Derby, any day!"

6

A special guest

Mandy was in the kitchen at Animal Ark, waiting for James to arrive. They were going round to Lilac Cottage to help Mandy's gran with her Spring Fair preparations. The Women's Institute was running a sweet stall there, and Gran had been busy making all sorts of toffee and fudge, which needed to be weighed and wrapped.

Mandy had also invited Mel along to help. If Mel kept busy, perhaps she wouldn't think so much about not being able to ride in the Donkey Derby.

Emily Hope came in from the surgery. "What a morning!" she said, filling the kettle and switching it on.

"Why, Mum?" Mandy asked. "Have you had lots of patients?"

"It felt like all the pets of Welford!" her mum replied, laughing. She made herself a mug of coffee, and sat down at the big pine table. "I must give Gran and Grandad a ring," she told Mandy. "Dad and I have been so busy without Simon around that we haven't seen them for ages. I thought they might like to come round for tea tomorrow," she explained.

"I'll ask them for you, if you like," Mandy offered. "I'm just waiting for James to arrive, then we're going round to Lilac Cottage. Gran has made loads of treacle toffee and fudge for the Spring Fair," Mandy explained. "And James, Mel and I are going round to help her."

Mrs Hope laughed. "*Eat* it, you mean!"

"Well, I think James is hoping for some free fudge," Mandy said, grinning. "But we're meant to be packing it in little pieces of paper and tying ribbons round them."

Emily Hope laughed again. "Well, I shouldn't take Blackie with you," she advised," or you might find yourselves with nothing to pack!"

"I think you're right, Mum. James is bad enough, but James *and* Blackie would be a total disaster!"

There was a knock on the kitchen door. "That'll be James," Mandy said, going over to let him in.

James's face was red; his hair was sticking to his forehead.

"You look hot!" Mandy said.

"I've been running," James explained.

Mandy laughed. "You can't wait to get at that toffee and fudge, James Hunter!" she said, with a grin. "We're off then, Mum!" Mandy called.

She and James walked down the garden path. "So you decided to leave Blackie at home, then?" Mandy asked, as they made their way towards Lilac Cottage.

"Mm. I thought he might try and eat your gran's sweets," James replied. Blackie could be very naughty at times.

Mandy laughed again. That's just what she and her mum had thought!

As they reached Lilac Cottage, Gran and Grandad were just arriving themselves, carrying big bags of shopping.

"Thank goodness we got here in time for you," Gran said. "There were queues in all the shops. I thought we were going to be late!"

"Hi, Gran! Hi, Grandad!" Mandy said, opening the gate for them.

"Hello, Mr and Mrs Hope," James said, politely. "Can we help you carry your shopping?"

Mandy giggled. "He's just hoping you'll reward him, Gran!"

Mandy's gran smiled at them both. "Well, I *do* have some walnut cookies," she told them.

"Wow!" said James, pushing his glasses further up on to his nose. "Walnut cookies *and* toffee and fudge!" He took two carrier bags full of shopping and began to stagger with them towards the back door of the cottage.

"See what I mean?" Mandy laughed, taking a bag herself.

"Well, it sounds a fair exchange to me," Grandad said. "I'm expecting some cookies too, after all this shopping!"

Mandy heard a screech of brakes, as Mel's borrowed bike came to a halt outside the gate of Lilac Cottage.

"Hi everyone!" said Mel. She pushed the bike through the gateway and up the path. "I'm looking forward to this." She grinned as she propped her bike against the cottage wall. "It sounds like a dream job!"

As they went into the kitchen, a delicious smell of fudge and toffee hit them. "Wow!" Mel exclaimed. "This is going to be even more fun than I thought!"

"I'm not really hungry," Mandy admitted, at teatime.

"Aha!" Adam Hope said, grinning as he lifted salad on to his plate. "I heard all about helping Gran with her toffee and fudge."

"We *did* help," Mandy said. "It's just that it seemed to involve eating as well!"

"They don't exactly starve you at Lilac Cottage, do they?" Emily Hope remarked, helping herself to new potatoes.

"Walnut cookies," Mandy explained. "Well . . . that was to start. Then we *had* to sample the different flavours of toffee and fudge we were packing—"

"Say no more," Mr Hope laughed.

"Well, I hope you get your appetite back for tomorrow's tea," Mrs Hope said.

"Oh, I'll eat lots then," Mandy replied. "Can James come too, please? And Mel?"

"I should think so," said Emily Hope, smiling.

Mandy was out in the Animal Ark garden the next afternoon, when Gran and Grandad arrived. They were a little early.

"Hello, dear," Gran said. "I was just telling Grandad that Mr Stevens is planning to give some of his lovely broad-bean crop to the Spring Fair fruit and vegetable stall. But Grandad doesn't want to pick his yet. He says it's too soon." Gran's eyes twinkled teasingly.

"Now, then, Dorothy," said Tom Hope, rubbing his chin, thoughtfully. "If the opposition is going to supply beans, then perhaps I should too."

"The opposition, Grandad?" Mandy asked. She looked puzzled as she gave her gran and grandad a hug.

Mandy's gran laughed. "Grandad and Mr Stevens are having a competition over their early broad beans – to see whose are ready to pick first," she explained.

The Stevenses lived in Jasmine Cottage, in the same road as Lilac Cottage. Mandy knew Paul Stevens, who was in James's class at school.

"Oh well," said Mandy," as long as we raise plenty of money at the Spring Fair, perhaps it doesn't matter where the beans come from!"

Gran and Grandad were still talking about

broad beans when Mel and James arrived, some time later. Mandy let them in eagerly. "Great! Thank goodness you're here," she said. "They're all talking about broad beans! Let's go into the office – I'll show you the final entry list Dad has prepared for the Donkey Derby." Mandy looked uneasily at Mel. "That's if you'd like to," she added.

Mel smiled. "That would be fun," she said. "Even though I'm not entering myself, I'm still interested."

In the Animal Ark office, Mandy opened the Donkey Derby folder. "Look," she said to James. "Rachel has entered Truffle. Rachel is in James's class," she explained to Mel. "Truffle sounds gorgeous."

Mandy told Mel about Maisie, Rachel's lurcher, and how she was expecting puppies a couple of days after the Spring Fair. "And Mrs Edwards' nephew George has also entered," Mandy added.

"There are loads more entries than last year," Mel said, looking at the sheet. "I wonder who's going to win?"

Adam Hope called to say that tea was

ready. The friends left the office and went through to the kitchen to sit down at the table, which was laid for seven. As her mum served out spaghetti to everyone, Mandy helped herself to some bread, her mind far away.

"You're quiet, love." Adam Hope looked across at Mandy as he twisted spaghetti around his fork.

"Hmm. I was just thinking," Mandy replied.

"I know that look," her dad said, grinning.

"There's a plan ticking away in there. And it usually involves animals! Come on, out with it."

"Lightning . . . and Raindrop," Mandy said, slowly. She looked at Mel. "It seems such a shame that they can't be at the Donkey Derby."

Mr Hope looked thoughtful. He carried on eating his spaghetti, but when he had cleared his plate he stood up from the table. "That was delicious, love," he said to Mrs Hope. "I could manage a little bit more, if there's any left! But I've just got to make a quick phone call first." He went out into the hall, closing the door behind him.

Mandy was still thinking about Lightning and Raindrop when her dad returned. He sat down at the table and beamed round at everyone.

"You look very pleased about something," Emily Hope said.

"I am," Adam Hope replied, digging into the last of the food. "I've just arranged for a very special guest to come to the Spring Fair on Saturday."

"Who is it, Dad?" Mandy asked. "Someone famous?"

Adam Hope grinned, his dark-brown eyes twinkling. "Oh yes," he replied, "she's famous around here, anyway. She's a champion runner!"

"Does she run for England?" Mel asked.

"Oh no!" Mr Hope replied. "Only for Welford. But she can't run at the moment. She's just had a baby . . ."

Mandy gasped. "Ooh, Dad! It's Lightning, isn't it – and Raindrop? They're coming!"

"Yes," said Mr Hope, looking pleased with himself. "I've just telephoned Mrs Dawkins at Glisterdale, and asked her if she'd like to bring Lightning and Raindrop to the Donkey Derby – as guests of honour."

Mandy, James and Mel looked at each other in delight.

"That's wonderful, Mr Hope," said Mel. "Lightning might not be able to race this year, but at least she won't be left out now. Thank you *very* much!"

7

The Spring Fair

Mandy woke up early on Saturday morning, the day of the Spring Fair. She jumped out of bed, padded over to her bedroom window and pulled back her curtains. *Thank goodness!* It wasn't raining.

Dressing quickly, she went downstairs. "Hi, Mum," she said. Mrs Hope had just finished setting the table and was putting sliced bread into the toaster.

"Mandy! You're up early," said Mrs Hope, smiling at her daughter. "I wonder why!"

"It's Fair day!" said Mandy, happily. "Dad said he could give James and me a lift to Glisterdale before he starts morning surgery. We're going to help Mel groom Lightning, ready for this afternoon. It's going to be great!"

"Well, have a good breakfast," Mrs Hope advised her. "It'll be a long morning. Shall I make you some sandwiches for lunch?"

"No, it's OK, Mum," Mandy replied. "Mrs Dawkins is giving us lunch before bringing us all down to the Fair."

"Fine," said Mrs Hope. "Let's just hope that Animal Ark doesn't get any call-outs this morning. Then your dad can get on with preparing for the Donkey Derby as soon as morning surgery is finished, while I see to the animals in the residential unit." Mrs Hope sighed. "Thank goodness Simon is back on Monday!"

Mr Hope poked his head around the kitchen door. "What time is James expecting us?" he asked.

Mandy looked at the clock on the wall. "In ten minutes' time, Dad," she replied, hastily spreading marmalade on to her toast. Popping the last bit of toast into her mouth as she went, Mandy rushed upstairs to brush her teeth and get her backpack.

"Ready, Dad!" she shouted a couple of minutes later, flying down the stairs two at a time.

"You're like a human whirlwind sometimes, Mandy!" Adam Hope said, laughing. "Let's go and pick up James."

Adam Hope dropped Mandy and James off at Glisterdale, saying he'd see them later at the Fair.

Mel was outside, waiting for them. "Hi, you two," she said, smiling. She had a cotton bag over her arm. "I've got the grooming things," she said, patting the bag. "Shall we get going?"

James hitched his glasses further up on to his nose. "This is going to be fun. I've never done this before."

As they all made their way to the stable block, Mel showed Mandy and James some neat's-foot oil that her gran had given her. "We can put it on with a paint-brush," she said.

"What do we use it for?" James asked.

"Painting Lightning's hooves," Mel explained. "It'll make her hooves look smart, and it's good for them too – once it's soaked in."

"We want them to look smart," Mandy agreed. "After all, Lightning's a star! No donkey has ever beaten her in the Donkey Derby."

"Until today," Mel sighed.

"But she still won't be beaten," James pointed out, "because she won't be racing."

"Mm, I suppose so," Mel replied quietly.

Lightning must have heard them approaching her stable. She pushed her head out of the opening in the stable door and brayed loudly.

"She's saying 'Come and get on with it!' "
James laughed.

"OK, Lightning," Mandy said, pushing up
her sleeves. "Let's get to work!"

Inside the stable, Mel took out the
grooming tools. She showed them what
needed to be done, then gave Mandy and
James a brush each. "The main thing to
remember," she added, seriously, "is to be
gentle with her."

"Yes," Mandy said. "It's hardly any time
since she had Raindrop."

Mandy and Mel concentrated on
Lightning's head and neck, brushing
carefully on either side. James brushed down
the donkey's back and hindquarters. Then,
with a metal, wide-toothed comb, Mel
combed through Lightning's short mane,
and the end of her tail.

Afterwards, Mel fetched a bowl of warm
water and a clean cloth, and began to bathe
Lightning's eyes gently.

"Is there anything in the water?" Mandy
asked her.

"Nothing fancy. Just a pinch of

bicarbonate of soda from Gran's kitchen cupboard," Mel replied, with a grin. "I borrowed a clean duster, too. We can give both of their coats a shine, when we've finished brushing Lightning."

When Lightning's coat was soft and silky, Mandy helped Mel to fit her head-collar and lead-rope, and they led her outside, leaving Raindrop in the stable. "Now for the neat's-foot oil," Mel said.

While Mandy held the lead-rope and James held the tin, Mel dipped a paint-brush into the oil and carefully painted Lightning's hooves. Then she stood back to admire her work. The hooves were gleaming in the morning sun.

"She looks great, Mel," Mandy said. "What about Raindrop?"

Mel shook her head. "We don't need to do anything to her," she said, "except a gentle rub with the duster. She doesn't need it. Lightning washes her!"

As they were all admiring Lightning, Mrs Dawkins came over from the house. "I've brought something for Raindrop," she said, holding up a small head-collar. "I bought it years ago, when I was showing one of my mares and her foal in the Welford Show."

"Oh, isn't it cute?" Mandy said. "It's so tiny!"

"I think it might still be a bit big for Raindrop," Mrs Dawkins said.

The head-collar, buckled on the tightest hole, fitted Raindrop loosely. Mandy helped Mel and James to give the foal and Lightning a last rub with the duster.

"They look wonderful," Joyce Dawkins told them. "Now, let's get them back into their stable while we have an early lunch."

Mel looked at her watch. "My goodness, we've been working on Lightning and Raindrop for ages! I can't believe it's lunch-time already."

"I can." James grinned. "We had an early start this morning, and my stomach is rumbling!"

After lunch, Mrs Dawkins slowly led Lightning, with Raindrop at her side, out of their stable and over to the horse box they were to travel in to the Fair. It was a big, solid old vehicle.

Mandy watched as Joyce Dawkins led Lightning up the ramp. She was surprised that Lightning was no trouble to load into the horse box. She knew that horses and donkeys often got very frightened when they had to walk up a steep ramp.

Raindrop followed her mum happily, but it was hard work for her spindly little legs to manage the steepness.

"Put an arm round her, someone," Joyce called. "Help her up."

Mandy stood by with James, ready to help, while Mel hurried forward. "Up you go, sweetie," she said, gently pushing on the foal's hindquarters. With a scrabble of tiny hooves, Raindrop managed to climb the ramp, and soon she and Lightning were safely in the straw-filled horse box.

"There we are!" said Joyce Dawkins.

Mrs Dawkins and Mel walked back down the wooden ramp, then Mrs Dawkins pushed it up and secured the doors.

"Good," said Mandy, breathing a sigh of

relief. "They're safely inside."

Mrs Dawkins went over to the stables to tell her assistant that they were about to leave. Mel went round to the front of the vehicle and climbed into the cab. "In you come, you two," she called, moving over to make room for Mandy and James.

"Wow! We're a long way up," James said. It was a tight squeeze with the three of them on the seat.

"Can we see Lightning and Raindrop from here?" asked Mandy.

"Yes. Through that little window behind you," Mel told her.

Mandy turned round and peered through the window. She could just see down into the dark depths of the horse box. Lightning was there, with Raindrop cuddled close to her side.

"Off we go!" said Mrs Dawkins as she climbed into the driving seat and started up the engine. She pulled away slowly and smoothly.

"We can see right over the hedges," Mandy

said with delight, as they trundled slowly towards Welford.

"*And* into people's gardens," James observed, as they reached the outskirts of the village.

"Look!" Mandy cried. "There's Gran, on her way to the village green." The three of them waved at Dorothy Hope, whose arms were full of bags and boxes.

A minute later, they arrived at the village green.

"Look! Over there!" Mandy pointed excitedly. "There's the big banner for the Donkey Derby!" There were already a few other horse boxes parked near the banner, with donkeys being led out of them.

"We'll aim for there, then, shall we?" said Mrs Dawkins. She steered carefully on to the village green, then parked near the other horse boxes.

Mandy had a last look through the window at the two donkeys before jumping out of the cab after James. Mel jumped down after her, and they ran round to the back of the horse box, where Mrs Dawkins was letting down the ramp.

Inside the box, Lightning's tail flicked. Raindrop turned to peer out, her eyes round with interest.

Mandy watched Mel walking up the ramp with her gran.

"Now you wait there, Mel," Mrs Dawkins said. "Just hold on to Raindrop's hindquarters a moment, while I undo Lightning."

Soon, Lightning was walking down the ramp. She was so excitable, that Mrs Dawkins had to hold her back!

"She thinks she's here to run, as usual!" Mrs Dawkins laughed. "Not this year, girl," she told the donkey, patting her side affectionately.

Mandy ran up to help Mel guide Raindrop down the slope, holding her gently on either side, with an arm round her chest and the other hand on her hindquarters. James waited at the bottom of the ramp, his arms held out to catch the foal in case she slipped.

"Phew!" said James, pushing back his

glasses, when both donkey and foal were on the ground. "I'm glad they're safely here, at last."

"Me too," said Mandy. "Lightning's really good at travelling in the box, isn't she?"

Mel nodded. "Gran leaves an old horse trailer in the field for the donkeys and horses," she explained. "When the weather's bad, some of them use it as a shelter. So they get used to going up the ramp into the horse box, too!"

"What a brilliant idea," said Mandy. She

thought for a moment. "And, of course, Raindrop will do what her mum does!"

Joyce Dawkins was busy carrying down bales of straw. Mel and James carried one down between them, while Mandy held Lightning's head-collar. Little Raindrop kept close to her mother, watching everything.

"Under the tree, I think," said Mrs Dawkins, carrying a bale over and dumping it in the shade of the old oak-tree. "That should give them plenty of shade."

Gradually, they carried all the bales of straw over to the tree to make a small, square enclosure for Lightning and Raindrop, two bales high. Joyce Dawkins then went back to the horse box to fetch water and food for Lightning. Soon, Lightning and Raindrop were settled comfortably.

"Raindrop looks so cute," Mandy said, leaning her elbows on the straw wall and gazing at mother and foal. "I hope Lightning has a good time, even though she has to stand by and watch this year."

Pony Rides
all proceeds to
Glisterdale Horse and
Pony Rescue Sanctuary

8
An emergency!

Leaving Mrs Dawkins at the enclosure, Mandy, James and Mel went to have a look round the Fair. At one end of the village green, there were a number of stalls and tables set up, belonging to all sorts of societies and organisations. Grandad was there manning the fruit and vegetable stall.

"Hello, Grandad!" Mandy called. "Have

you got any broad beans for sale, today?" she asked, grinning.

"I certainly have, young lady!" her grandfather replied. "The best on offer are from Lilac Cottage's garden, of course. But I do have a few others, as well!" he said with a twinkle in his eye, as Mr Stevens walked up to the stall.

At the WI stall, Gran was arranging the fudge and toffee they'd packaged for her, alongside other goodies made by other members.

"Goodness, that coconut ice looks yummy," said Mel.

Mandy nodded, then spotted a familiar shape further down the green. "Oh, look! It's Paul – and Paddy!" She set off across the grass towards Paul Stevens and Paddy, his Exmoor pony. James and Mel followed.

"Hi, Paul!" Mandy said. "And how are you, Paddy?" she said softly, to his pony. "Paul chose Paddy from Glisterdale," Mandy told Mel.

"And Mel is Mrs Dawkins's granddaughter," James explained to Paul.

"Paddy's looking fantastic – really glossy!" Mandy said. She turned to James. "Remember what Paddy was like when we first saw him?"

James nodded, and told Mel how, when Paddy had arrived at Glisterdale, he'd had scars and sores all over him. He had been badly neglected and whipped by his previous owner.

"Paul worked so hard to make him well again," Mandy added. Paul looked pleased.

"What are you doing here?" James asked Paul.

Paul showed them the sign he had painted. On the board was written:

PONY RIDES
all proceeds to
Glisterdale Horse and Pony Rescue
Sanctuary

"That's a brilliant idea!" Mandy beamed. Then she looked a little worried. "Paddy won't get too tired, will he?" she asked anxiously.

Paul shook his head. "Oh, I won't let that happen," he told her. "It won't be a very long ride, and I've decided that I'll take his saddle off after every five rides. Then I'll let him eat the grass, over there by the hedge."

"Oh, that's good," Mandy said, smiling at him. "Then he won't get bored, either."

"That's what I thought," said Paul. He rubbed Paddy's ears and stroked his neck happily. He grinned at Mandy. "This looks like my first customer coming," he said, as a small child approached, holding out some coins.

Just then, the loudspeaker crackled into life, and Mr Hope's voice came booming out. "Good afternoon. Could all entrants for the Donkey Derby make their way to the registration table, please? Thank you!"

Mandy, James and Mel hurried over to help. Mandy's heart soared with excitement as she saw donkeys being led towards the table where her father was waiting. She could see Rachel Lowe at the head of the queue. Beside her stood a sweet, dark-coloured donkey, looking around at everything with her long ears pricked, but staying quietly by Rachel.

"Oh, good! I'm glad you're here," Adam Hope said, as they arrived. He handed the list of entrants to Mandy. "You can mark off each donkey and owner as they arrive, Mandy," he said. "And write in their number." He pointed to a pile of numbered cards and safety pins. "James – you can give out the numbers to the owners. And Mel – you can help the owners pin the numbers on."

"Hi, Rachel," Mandy said, cheerfully, to the first entrant in the queue.

Rachel smiled at her. "Come on, Truffle," she said, tugging gently at the lead-rope. Doing as she was told, Truffle stepped forward. She blew inquisitively at Mandy's notes.

Mandy giggled as the sheets of paper scattered. "Watch out, Truffle!" She laughed. "Otherwise, we'll be muddling up all the owners and donkeys!" Mandy gathered up

83

the sheets and clipped them together.

Truffle gazed at Mandy from her large, brown eyes. "She's gorgeous," Mandy said, looking down the list for Rachel's entry. Mandy smiled at Rachel. "You're number nine," she told her, ticking them off on the list.

"Thanks," said Rachel, taking the number card from James. Mel helped her pin the card to the back of her shirt.

Mandy thought Rachel seemed a little uneasy. "How is Maisie?" she asked.

Rachel tried to smile, but her freckled face looked worried. "My mum's at home with her, but—"

"Move them along, Mandy," Mr Hope called. "We've got a lot to check."

Mandy smiled at Rachel. "I'm sure she'll be fine," she said, reassuringly. "Good luck!" she called. Then she turned her attention to the next entrant.

What lovely animals donkeys are, Mandy thought, as she watched them looking around with interest or lowering their shaggy heads to chew at the grass as they waited. About half the entrants had been registered now. Once registered, Mr Hope checked that the donkeys were fit to run.

Most of the donkeys were grey, but there were two chocolate-brown ones in the queue. There was also a sleek black donkey, which threw his head up and brayed loudly as Mandy watched.

Owners chatted, and their donkeys touched noses. Sometimes they squealed; sometimes they just flicked their tails and snorted.

"George Edwards," said the next entrant, grinning at Mandy. Beside him stood the big, black donkey.

Mandy looked down the list. "From Monkton Spinney," she said, "and your donkey's name is . . . Scary." She looked up at the boy, questioningly. "He's not, is he? Scary, I mean."

The boy laughed. "When I got him, he was so thin and tatty, he looked like a big black scarecrow," he explained. He looked at his donkey, proudly. "He looks better now," he added.

"I can see that you look after him," Mandy said.

"Mandy!" Adam Hope called. "We must keep them moving." He winked at George Edwards. "You can't chat to every entrant," he said to his daughter, "or we won't have time for the actual race!"

"Sorry, Dad," Mandy said, grinning. She turned to the next boy in the queue.

"John Blithwaite," the boy said.

"And your donkey's name is Pickles," Mandy said, adding with a grin, "or is it Tiddles?"

When there were no more donkeys waiting to be registered and checked over, Mr Hope said he could manage the few late arrivals himself. Mandy, James and Mel made their way back over to Lightning and Raindrop's enclosure. The two donkeys were surrounded by a crowd of admirers. Mandy was about to edge her way through the crowd when she noticed Rachel Lowe

hurrying out of the Donkey Derby entrants'
area. She was looking very worried.

"Oh dear, I wonder what's up," Mandy
said to James. "Let's see if we can help."

"Rachel!" Mandy called, as she, James and
Mel ran over to her. "What's the matter? Is
it Maisie?" Mandy could see that Rachel
was close to tears.

Rachel nodded. "I shouldn't have left
her!" she said. "I shouldn't have come!"

"Why, what's happened?" Mandy asked.

"Dad's just come to tell me that Maisie's

trying to have her pups now – and she's in trouble," Rachel explained. "He knew I'd want to be there with Maisie. He's staying here to look after Truffle." Rachel tried to hold back a sob. "Dad said your mum is on her way over to help." Tears were now falling down Rachel's cheeks.

Mandy turned pale. "Quick, Rachel, you must go," she said. "James and I will help your dad with Truffle." She gave Rachel a small push. "Leave it all to us!"

9
A new rider

As Rachel hurried away, Mandy, James and Mel rushed over to Truffle, who was being looked after by Mr Lowe. He looked worried. "It's such a shame," he said, running his fingers through his dark, curly hair. "Rachel was so looking forward to the Donkey Derby. But it's more important that she's with Maisie now. Rachel thinks the world of that dog." He rubbed his chin thoughtfully. "I just hope she'll be all right."

"Try not to worry, Mr Lowe," Mandy said. "My mum will know what to do."

Mr Lowe smiled. "I'd best take Truffle home, I suppose," he said. "And I think she was enjoying the excitement of the Derby, too!"

"Shall I go and cross Truffle off the registration list?" James asked Mandy.

"Not just yet," Mandy replied. James looked at her curiously. Mandy had a faraway sound to her voice . . .

"Mr Lowe," she said, "Truffle could still have the fun of the race, you know."

Rachel's dad looked at Mandy curiously. "How do you mean?" he asked.

"Well," Mandy replied, "there's someone else here who might like to ride her . . ." She looked at Mel.

Mel's eyes widened in surprise, then she nodded enthusiastically.

Breathlessly, Mandy began to explain. "Mel was going to ride Lightning, you see, and then she couldn't, and – I just wondered," she hesitated. Then, quickly, she said, "I don't suppose you'd let *Mel* ride Truffle in the race?"

A big grin spread over Mr Lowe's face. "That's a great idea, Mandy. Rachel's been practising with Truffle all week. She'll be tickled pink if Truffle gets to race, after all!" He looked at Mel. "So, Mel, are you keen?"

Mel beamed at Mr Lowe and then at Mandy. "You bet!" she said, her eyes shining. "Let's go and tell my gran!"

As they were making their way over to Mrs Dawkins, the speaker system crackled into life again. Adam Hope's voice boomed out another announcement. "Hello again, everyone," he said. "In half an hour's time, the Donkey Derby will begin. Will any late entrants please make their way to the registration area, to register and be checked over by the vet. Thank you."

"We'd better get cracking," said Mr Lowe, giving Rachel's hard hat to Mel. Then he handed over Truffle's lead-rope to her. "You have a chat with Truffle – get to know her – while I go over to my van and fetch the tack."

"And James and I will go over and tell your gran what's happening," Mandy said.

"Good thinking, Mandy," James said, as they walked over to Lightning and Raindrop's enclosure. He chuckled. "I could tell from the look on your face back there, that you were hatching some kind of idea!"

Mrs Dawkins was delighted at the news and, when Mandy and James went over to tell him, Mr Hope said the change of rider was fine.

They made their way back over to Mel. Truffle's liquid brown eyes looked a little surprised as Mel walked her up and down, talking to her. "We're both going to race in the Donkey Derby, after all!" she told the donkey. Truffle pricked her ears forward.

"How are you two getting on?" Mr Lowe asked. "We haven't got much time."

"Oh, I think we're going to be just fine, Mr Lowe." Mel smiled.

Mandy held Truffle while Mel and Mr

Lowe put on the saddle and bridle. Truffle turned her head, and nudged Mel as she tightened the girth.

"I think she likes you," Geoff Lowe commented. "Now, up you go," he added.

Mandy kept hold of Truffle's bridle while Mel put her left foot into the stirrup iron. She was about to climb into the saddle when Mr Lowe put out a restraining hand. "Stop!" he said. "You can't ride in those sandals, lass. It wouldn't be safe!"

Mel looked down at her feet, then across at Mandy. "I was so excited," she said, "I didn't think. You're right!"

Mandy bit her lip. She hadn't thought about that, either, when she'd rushed to suggest that Mel could ride Truffle. If Mel was disappointed again, it would be her fault!

Mandy looked guiltily down at her own feet. Then suddenly her face lit up. "Mel!" she said, excitedly. "Look at *my* shoes!"

Mel looked at Mandy's feet, her face puzzled.

Mandy grinned. "I'm wearing the right

footwear!" she said. It was true. Mandy was wearing strong, lace-up trainers.

Mel still looked disappointed. "*You* can ride Truffle, then," she said.

"No, silly," Mandy said. "Your feet look about the same size as mine. We can change shoes!" She started undoing the laces in her trainers. "Quick! Take those sandals off!"

The loudspeaker boomed again. "Ten minutes to go for the Donkey Derby," came Adam Hope's voice. "Will all entrants begin making their way to the starting line, please."

Mandy's heart was pounding. Would they be in time?

"Don't look now," James warned them. "But I think someone is coming over to say hello."

"Oh no!" Mandy gasped, as she turned round. Coming towards them was Mrs Ponsonby, with Pandora, her Pekinese dog, under her arm. She never went anywhere without Pandora.

Mrs Ponsonby was possibly the nosiest person in Welford. She liked to know everything about everyone. She was in a chatty mood, as always. "Hello!" she called. "What on earth are you two girls doing?"

Mandy moved over to one side. "Hello, Mrs Ponsonby," she said, hopping about as she pulled off her left sock to hand it over to Mel. "Well—"

"The Fair seems to be going well," Mrs Ponsonby continued, not waiting for an answer to her question. The cherries on the side of her large sunhat wobbled as she spoke. Mrs Ponsonby was well-known for her large and outrageous hats, and at any other time Mandy and Mel would have been trying hard not to laugh, but today they had other things on their mind.

"It's great," Mandy agreed, breathlessly, as she crammed her foot into one of Mel's sandals. It felt like her feet were actually a size bigger than Mel's.

"It is," Mrs Ponsonby agreed. "But we can't stop now. Pandora and I are on our way to see the Donkey Derby," she explained. She swept away to find a place at the front of the crowd that was gathering near the starting line.

Moments later, Mel was up on Truffle, gently walking her up and down. The sound system gave its familiar crackle, and Adam Hope's voice announced the final call for entrants to join the starting line.

"This is it!" said Mel. "Wish us luck."

Mandy watched Mel trot Truffle over towards the starting line. But, as they arrived in front of Mr Hope, Mandy saw him point to Rachel's shirt and shake his head. Mandy clapped a hand to her mouth. "Her number!" she said. "She's forgotten her number!"

"Quick, here you are," Mr Lowe said to Mandy, reaching into his pocket. "Rachel left it with me."

Mandy grabbed the number card, and ran as fast as Mel's sandals would let her. "Wait, just a minute, Dad, please," she shouted. "Here it is. Mel's number!"

Mr Hope signalled for Mandy to come over quickly. "Just in time." He grinned.

Mel turned round, a look of relief on her face. "Oh, thank goodness! Your dad said he'd have to disqualify me if I didn't have Truffle's registration number!"

"Bend down," Mandy said. "I'll pin it on for you."

Mel leaned down while Mandy pinned the card to Mel's shirt. "Thanks, Mandy," she said, "you're a pal!"

When Mel had urged Truffle into line with the other donkeys, Adam Hope raised his arm and fired the starting gun. They were off!

As the donkeys leaped away and the cheering began, James arrived beside Mandy. "Listen!" he said.

Ee haw! Ee haw! Eee haaaw!

The sound came from behind them. "I know who *that* is!" Mandy said, grinning, as she turned round. Then she grabbed James's arm. "Look!" she shouted.

James turned to where Mandy was pointing. They both watched open-mouthed.

From Lightning and Raindrop's straw-bale enclosure, a flash of grey leaped out, over the bales of straw, and galloped after the other donkeys in the Derby.

All around, people were cheering and shouting. But the cheers weren't for George Edwards, who was in the lead on his big black donkey, Scary. Everyone was cheering for Lightning!

Mandy and James watched, spellbound, as Lightning galloped on, her painted hooves glinting in the sunlight. She was gaining on the other donkeys all the time.

"Quick," said Mandy to James. "Let's get over to the finishing line!"

They rushed across the green, where more people were waiting at the end of the racetrack, ready to see the winner flash first over the line. Mrs Ponsonby had found herself a place at the front. The cherries were almost bouncing off her hat, she was cheering so loudly.

"Look at Mel and Truffle!" Mandy was jumping up and down with excitement. "They're in second place!" she said. She could see that George Edwards on Scary was still in first place, with Mel and Truffle close behind. A short way behind Truffle was a small grey donkey, which Mandy recognised as Pickles, ridden by John Blithwaite.

Mandy could see Mel leaning forward in the saddle to talk to Truffle, urging her on. Truffle pricked her ears, then galloped past George Edwards and Scary.

"Oh, well done, Mel!" Mandy called. "Truffle's in the lead!"

"But look who's coming!" said James.

Galloping down the track came the riderless Lightning, her hooves flying. She passed Scary, and then she was alongside Truffle.

The two donkeys galloped under the "Finish" banner. "She's won!" Mandy cried.

10

The winner

A deafening cheer rose up from the crowd. "But *who* won?" James asked. "Truffle or Lightning?"

As they watched, Lightning slowed down to a canter. Then, without stoping, she simply turned round and trotted happily back over to the straw-bale enclosure and her baby, which caused even more clapping and laughter.

"It was Lightning," Mandy replied. "But Lightning couldn't win, could she? She wasn't being ridden – *and* she wasn't entered."

They hurried over to the enclosure, where Joyce Dawkins was busy putting a rug over Lightning.

"Did you see her, James, as she came past the finish?" Mandy said, laughing as they ran. "She was smiling. She really was!"

James laughed, too. "She looked very pleased with herself, didn't she?" he agreed.

Mandy saw her dad also making his way over to the enclosure. He pushed through the onlookers to reach Lightning. "Let's have a look at her," he said. Quickly his eyes looked the donkey over, and he felt down her sides and legs. "She seems fine," he said, ruffling her forelock.

He turned to Joyce Dawkins. "I reckon Lightning's milk will give young Raindrop a few hiccups, tonight!" he said, with a chuckle. "Glad to see you've got a rug for her." Then he hurried back to his race organiser's tent.

"Now we know that Lightning's all right, let's go and congratulate Mel," Mandy suggested. They made their way over to Mel, who was also surrounded by a crowd.

But when she saw Mandy, Mel beckoned them over. "Is Lightning OK?" she asked anxiously.

Mandy smiled and nodded. "Dad's just checked her," she replied.

"Whew!" Mel gasped.

"You did really well," Mandy told her. "That was a brilliant race!"

"She certainly did," said Mr Lowe, beaming. "Well done, love. I'm sure Rachel will be thrilled."

Mel's face was pink with excitement. "Truffle was great, wasn't she?" she said, patting the donkey's dark-brown neck. She jumped down from the saddle and began to undo the girth strap. Then she took off the saddle and laid a rug that Mr Lowe handed her over the donkey's back. "Truffle's a great little donkey," she told him.

The loudspeaker system crackled again and Adam Hope's voice boomed out.

"Well, ladies and gentlemen, we've had a very exciting Donkey Derby this year – with a well-known gatecrasher!" Everyone laughed, and Mr Hope's voice continued. "I can announce the winner, now – Miss Melanie Dawkins, riding Rachel Lowe's Truffle. A last-minute change of rider. Well done to both of you!"

Mandy and James patted Mel on the back. "We'd better go now and help your gran with Lightning," Mandy said.

Mel nodded, gratefully.

"Poor girl," Mandy said softly in Lightning's ear, a couple of minutes later. "You thought you'd won, didn't you? Never mind – you can win next year."

"And what have you got to say for yourself?" Joyce Dawkins asked her donkey.

"She's not a bit sorry," Mandy said, laughing. "Shall we rub her down?" she asked.

"Let's leave it for a little while," Mrs Dawkins replied. "The rug will keep her warm." She pointed over to the little foal. "I think Raindrop is waking up for a feed," she explained.

They watched as Raindrop slowly stretched, then straightened her front legs, and clambered up on to all fours. The still-sleepy foal tottered over to nuzzle her mother and began to drink Lightning's milk.

Mandy heard voices. "Ahh!" said one. "How sweet!" said another. "That's the runaway donkey," said a third. Looking up, Mandy saw that the straw-bale enclosure was surrounded by onlookers. They were all gazing at Lightning and Raindrop. Mrs

Ponsonby was among them. Her cherry sunhat wobbled as she spoke to Pandora. "Well now, look at that, Pandora," she said. "One minute she's running in the Donkey Derby and the next she's feeding her baby!"

11

Rogues and pupils

11
Rosettes and puppies

Mandy, Mel and James were stretched out on the grass under the big oak-tree. Lightning and Raindrop were dozing, around the other side of the tree, in their enclosure. Truffle was happily grazing close by, where Mel had tethered her.

The loudspeaker crackled into action once more. "Ladies and gentlemen," Adam

Hope's voice announced, "the awarding of the winners' prizes and rosettes for the Donkey Derby will take place in five minutes' time, beside the starting line of the race. But I have been asked to make a special announcement." Mandy could tell from her dad's voice that he was smiling. "This year, we have had an extra, unofficial winner. So we have decided to award an extra rosette – to Lightning, owned by Joyce Dawkins of Glisterdale Horse and Pony Rescue Sanctuary. Lightning, as we all know, is here with her foal, Raindrop!"

The crowd let out a great cheer. "Wow!" said Mandy. "That's brilliant!"

Mel jumped up. "I'll untie Truffle," she offered. She looked around. "I wonder where Mr Lowe is," she added. "I expect he'll want to take Truffle into the ring."

"I'm sure he won't," Mandy said firmly. She grinned at Mel. "*You* won the race – you and Truffle."

Mel turned pink and looked pleased. "I'll take Truffle and go to find Mr Lowe, just to make sure," she said.

Mandy and James went round to the other side of the tree. Inside the enclosure, Mrs Dawkins was giving Lightning a quick brush-down. "Oh good, you're here," she said, when she saw them. "I didn't know where you'd gone." She smiled at them. "I'd like you two to do something for me," she said. She handed Lightning's lead-rope to Mandy. "I want you to take Lightning to collect her rosette," she said. "And you, James," she added, handing him the lead-rope which was attached to Raindrop's tiny head-collar, "make sure that Raindrop follows behind!"

Mandy and James looked at each other and grinned. "Thanks, Mrs Dawkins," Mandy said, her eyes shining.

James pushed his glasses up a bit on his nose, looking pleased. "Come on, Raindrop," he said. "You're going to see your mum get a special rosette!"

Mandy and James led Lightning and Raindrop through the crowd and over to the starting line. Mel was there, riding Truffle; George Edwards was there on Scary;

and John Blithwaite, on Pickles.

First, Mr Hope called up the donkey and rider who'd come third – John Blithwaite. He was given his green rosette. Then it was the turn of George Edwards, who collected the blue rosette for second place. Mel came next on Truffle. To loud cheers, she collected the winner's red rosette and cup.

When Lightning's name was called, Mandy led the donkey into the ring, followed by James with Raindrop. They made their way up to the prizegiving table, where the rosettes and prizes were laid out.

Mandy found herself standing in front of her dad. Smiling broadly, Adam Hope handed a purple rosette to his daughter. Mandy tied the rosette on to Lightning's leather halter, and the whole crowd burst into laughter and cheers.

Adam Hope then signalled to Mr Hunter in the officials' tent, and music blared out from the loudspeaker. It was time for the winners' parade. As Mandy led Lightning around the ring, she whispered into Lightning's ear, "You know all about this, don't you, girl? You're used to coming first – but today is special. You've never had Raindrop with you before!"

Lightning walked daintily beside Mandy, with her head held high. Mandy grinned happily. Lightning had won her rosette, after all. And Mel had won the Donkey Derby!

Outside the ring, Mandy said goodbye to George Edwards and John Blithwaite as they led Scary and Pickles away. Mel jumped off Truffle's back, and led her beside Mandy and James with Lightning and Raindrop.

As they all made their way back to the straw-bale enclosure, Mandy saw Rachel Lowe running towards them.

"Rachel! Is everything all right?" Mandy asked. "How is Maisie?"

Rachel was breathless. "Your mum had to do an emergency operation," she panted.

"Not at your house?" Mandy asked.

Rachel shook her head. "It was quite frightening," she said, looking serious. "Maisie had had one puppy, but she just couldn't get the next one out by herself. It was so big, it was stuck! Maisie was in an awful state. Your mum rushed us all back to Animal Ark – even the first puppy." Rachel looked proud. "I had to hold the puppy, all wrapped up, to keep it warm. And then your mum gave Maisie an anaesthetic, cut her open, got the two pups out, and then stitched her up again!"

"And Maisie's OK?" asked Mandy again.

"She's fine," Rachel replied, smiling broadly. "And Mum says I can keep the pup that came first!"

"That's brilliant," said Mandy. "And look at Truffle's rosette!"

Rachel's eyes opened wide. "First prize!" she said. "But how—"

"Your dad said that Mel could ride her," Mandy explained. "And she won!"

Rachel put her arms round her donkey's neck. "Truffle, you clever girl!" she said. She looked across at Mel and smiled. "Thanks so much for riding her for me," she said.

"I loved it," Mel admitted, handing over the reins to Rachel. "Trouble is, now I've got to give her back!"

Rachel leaned her head against Truffle's neck. "It's been an amazing day," she said, sighing with happiness. "Three pups for Maisie — and a red rosette for Truffle!"

"It certainly has," Mandy agreed, looking across at James and Mel. "We've had a great day, too — the best ever Welford Spring Fair!"

Mandy felt a nudge as Lightning pushed a soft muzzle into her hand. "Oh yes, Lightning," Mandy added, laughing. "It's been the most exciting Donkey Derby, as well!"

Ee haw! agreed Lightning. *Ee haw! Ee haw! Eee haaaw!*

HEDGEHOG HOME
Animal Ark Pets 14

Lucy Daniels

Mandy Hope loves animals and knows lots about them too – both her parents are vets! So Mandy's always able to help her friends with their pet problems . . .

Gran and Grandad Hope are looking after a friend's house over the winter. After a freezing night Mandy and Grandad discover a burst water pipe. And, out in the garden, the flood has destroyed Harold the hedgehog's nest. The garden is too frozen and snowy for Harold to build another home. Can Mandy find him a new one?

LUCY DANIELS
Animal Ark Pets

0 340 67283 8	Puppy Puzzle	£3.50	☐
0 340 67284 6	Kitten Crowd	£3.50	☐
0 340 67285 4	Rabbit Race	£3.50	☐
0 340 67286 2	Hamster Hotel	£3.50	☐
0 340 68729 0	Mouse Magic	£3.50	☐
0 340 68730 4	Chick Challenge	£3.50	☐
0 340 68731 2	Pony Parade	£3.50	☐
0 340 68732 0	Guinea-pig Gang	£3.50	☐
0 340 71371 2	Gerbil Genius	£3.50	☐
0 340 71372 0	Duckling Diary	£3.50	☐
0 340 71373 9	Lamb Lessons	£3.50	☐
0 340 71374 7	Doggy Dare	£3.50	☐
0 340 71375 5	Cat Crazy	£3.50	☐
0 340 73605 4	Pets' Party	£3.50	☐

All Hodder Children's books are available at your local bookshop, or can be ordered direct from the publisher. Just tick the titles you would like and complete the details below. Prices and availability are subject to change without prior notice.

Please enclose a cheque or postal order made payable to *Bookpoint Ltd*, and send to: Hodder Children's Books, 39 Milton Park, Abingdon, OXON OX14 4TD, UK. Email Address: orders@bookpoint.co.uk

If you would prefer to pay by credit card, our call centre team would be delighted to take your order by telephone. Our direct line *01235 400414* (lines open 9.00 am–6.00 pm Monday to Saturday, 24 hour message answering service). Alternatively you can send a fax on *01235 400454*.

TITLE		FIRST NAME		SURNAME	

ADDRESS	

DAYTIME TEL:		POST CODE	

If you would prefer to pay by credit card, please complete:
Please debit my Visa/Access/Diner's Card/American Express (delete as applicable) card no:

Signature .... Expiry Date: ....

If you would NOT like to receive further information on our products please tick the box. ☐